Dear Parents,

Welcome to the Scholastic Reader series. We have taken over 60 years of experience with teachers, parents, and children and put it into a program that is designed to match your child's interests and skills.

Level 1—Short sentences and stories made up of words kids can sound out using their phonics skills and words that are important to remember.

Level 2—Longer sentences and stories with words kids need to know and new "big" words that they will want to know.

Level 3—From sentences to paragraphs to longer stories, these books have large "chunks" of texts and are made up of a rich vocabulary.

Level 4—First chapter books with more words and fewer pictures.

It is important that children learn to read well enough to succeed in school and beyond. Here are ideas for reading this book with your child:

- Look at the book together. Encourage your child to read the title and make a prediction about the story.
- Read the book together. Encourage your child to sound out words when appropriate. When your child struggles, you can help by providing the word.
- Encourage your child to retell the story. This is a great way to check for comprehension.
- Have your child take the fluency test on the last page to check progress.

Scholastic Readers are designed to support your child's efforts to learn how to read at every age and every stage. Enjoy helping your child learn to read and love to read.

—**Francie Alexander**
Chief Education Officer
Scholastic Education

For Maria and Nicholas
—J.P.

For Shirley and Richard
—J.S.

Text copyright © 1994 by James Preller.
Illustrations copyright © 1994 by Jeffrey Scherer.
Activities copyright © 2003 Scholastic Inc.

Library of Congress Cataloging-in-Publication Data is available.

ISBN 0-590-47500-2

20 19 18 17 16 15 14 13   05 06 07

Printed in the U.S.A.   23

First printing, February 1994

Wake Me in Spring

by James Preller

Illustrated by Jeffrey Scherer

Scholastic Reader — Level 2

Cartwheel
·B·O·O·K·S· ®

SCHOLASTIC INC.

New York   Toronto   London   Auckland   Sydney
Mexico City   New Delhi   Hong Kong   Buenos Aires

Mouse looked out
from his hole and said,
"It's getting cold."
He shivered.

Bear scratched his belly
and yawned.

"Yes," said Bear.
"I feel winter in my bones."

Bear looked at the calendar.
"Time for bed!" he said.
"I'm so tired.
I will surely sleep
all winter long."

"But Bear,"
Mouse cried,
"you'll miss
winter!"

Bear yawned and said,
"I'm so sleepy. I don't care."

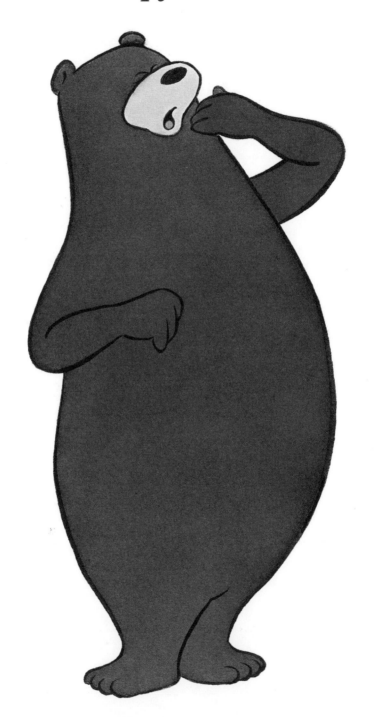

Mouse waved his arms.

"You will miss sleigh rides
in the snow!" said Mouse.

Bear rubbed his eyes and said,
"I'm so sleepy. I don't care."

"You will miss
hot chocolate
in steaming cups,"
said Mouse.

Bear pulled the curtains.
"I don't care," he said.

"You will miss ice skates on frozen lakes," said Mouse.

Bear locked the front door and said, "I don't care."

"You will miss snowmen with carrot noses!" cried Mouse.

Bear only sighed and said, "I don't care."

Mouse didn't say a word.

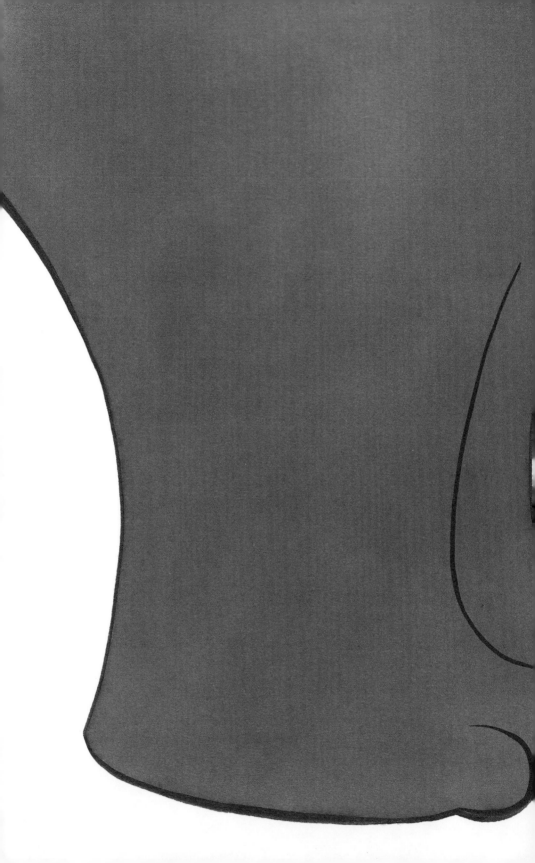

Finally, in a
sad, soft voice,
Mouse said,

"And I will
miss you."

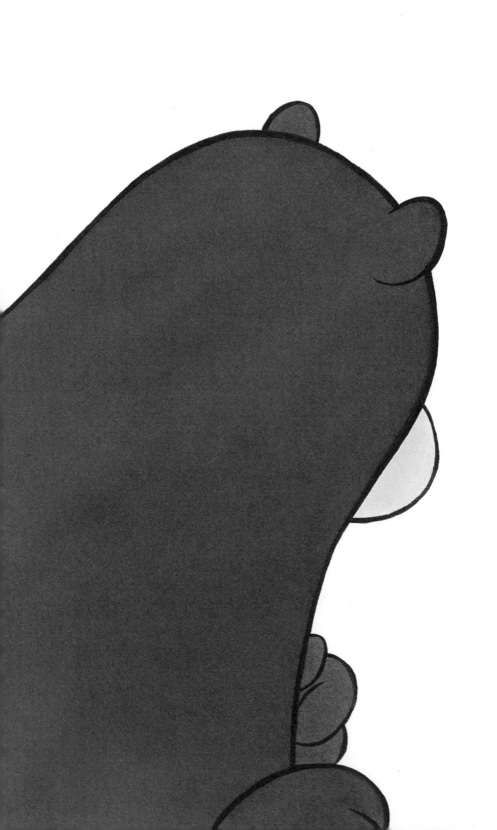

Bear
looked
into
Mouse's
watery
eyes.

Bear said, "Mouse,
I will not miss

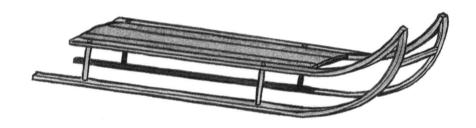

sleigh rides in the snow,

hot chocolate
in steaming
cups,

ice skates on frozen lakes,

or even snowmen
with carrot noses.

But I will
miss you.
I will miss you
very much."

Bear bent down
and gave his friend
the kind of hug
that bears give best . . .

. . . a hug that
lasts all
winter.

"My little friend,"
Bear explained,
"please understand.
A bear needs to sleep
all winter long."

Mouse sniffed and
blew his nose. *Kerhonk!*

Bear brushed his teeth
and said, "Mouse,
I feel winter
in my bones.

Please wake me
in spring
when flowers bloom
and birds sing."

Mouse tucked Bear
into bed and whispered,
"Good night, Bear.
Sleep tight.

I'll see you
in spring
when
flowers
bloom . . .

. . . and best friends sing!"